Is It Really Nearly CHRISTMAS?

Joyce Dunbar

Victoria Turnbull

Hodder
Children's
Books

Lucas looked out of the window. "Brrrr," he shivered, "it's cold."

"That's because it's winter," said Willow.

"It's dark," said Lucas.

"That's because it's night," said Willow.

"Will the night be over soon?" asked Lucas.

"It will," said Willow, "but this isn't just any old night. This is a magic night."

"Why is it magic?" asked Lucas.

"Because," whispered Willow,
"it's nearly Christmas!"

"Only nearly?" said Lucas. "Can't we
make Christmas come now?"

"We have to wait a little bit longer," said Willow.
"But we could play a remembering game
while we wait."

"What's remembering?" asked Lucas.

"Well," said Willow,
"do you remember when
we made paper chains?"

"I do," laughed Lucas,
"because Toby tried to
run away with them."

"And Puss chased after him," said Willow.

"What else did we do?" asked Lucas.

"We helped Mum decorate the tree,"
said Willow.

"And we put a fairy on top," added Lucas.

"We made presents for Toby and Puss,"
said Willow.

"And put them under the tree!"
said Lucas.

"We went out into the snow," said Willow.

"And put food out for the robin," said Lucas.

"We lit a Christmas candle,"
whispered Willow.

"That made shadows," murmured Lucas.
"What happens now?"

Willow thought for a moment.
"Lucas, what are you wearing?"

"My starry sleepsuit," said Lucas.

"And where will you sleep?"
asked Willow.

"In my bed," he replied.

"So, on this cold, dark night, we are warm in our pyjamas and we'll be tucked up in our cosy beds."

"You with your bear, me with Floppy Bunny," said Lucas. "What else?"

Willow held on to Lucas tightly.
"Look at the moon. The moon is waiting too.
And while it waits it shines."

"It does," said Lucas.

"And look at the stars. They are waiting too.
And while they wait they twinkle."

"Tell me some more!" said Lucas.

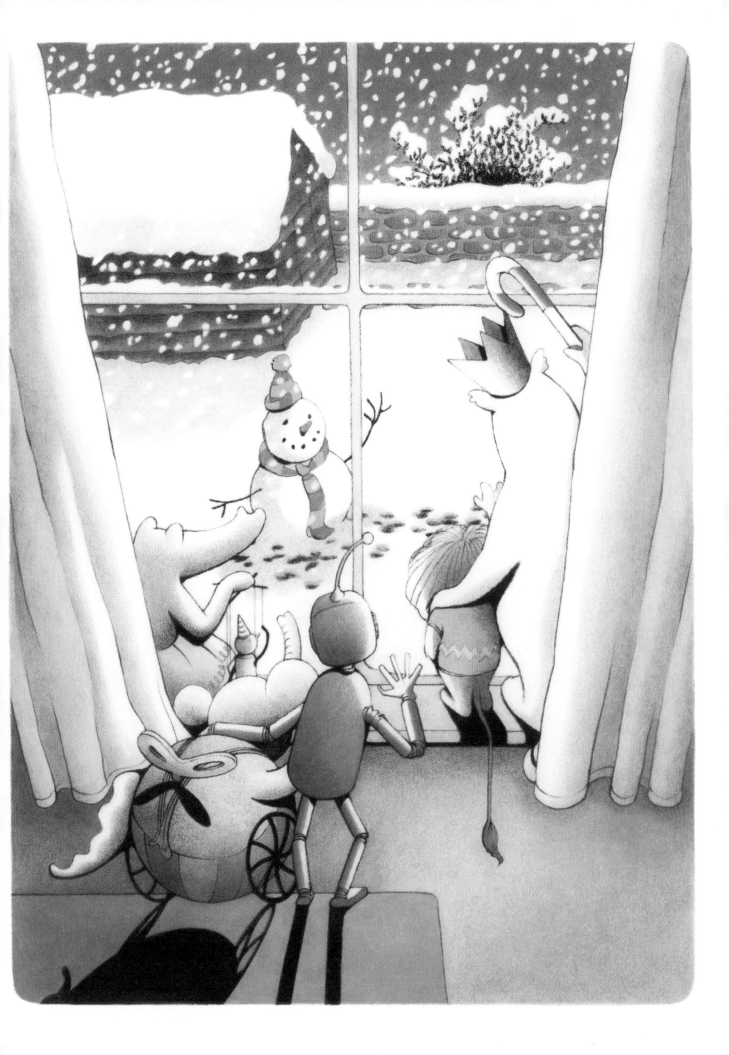

"You see these empty Christmas stockings at
the end of our beds? When we wake up in the
morning, they'll have presents in them."

"Oooh," said Lucas, "can't you make the
morning come faster?"

"It will come faster if we go to sleep," said Willow.

"I don't want to go to sleep," frowned Lucas.
"I want to wait and shine like the moon.
I want to watch and twinkle like the stars.
I want to see the magic."

"We can try," said Willow.

"How?" asked Lucas.

"You be the stars," said Willow, "and I'll be the moon."

"How?" asked Lucas.

"Keep your eyes wide open. And keep very still. We mustn't blink. One blink and we'll miss the magic."

Lucas sat on his bed, holding Floppy Bunny in his arms. He kept his eyes wide open. He tried not to blink. He tried his best to twinkle.

Willow stared into space. She kept her eyes wide open. She tried not to blink. She tried her hardest to shine.

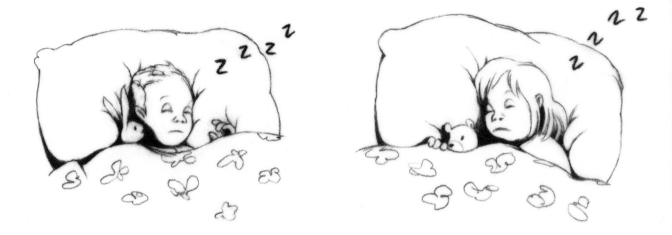

Lucas's eyelids began to flutter. So did Willow's.

His arms felt tired. So did Willow's.

YAWN went Lucas.
YAWN went Willow.

Lucas flopped. Willow drooped.

"Snuffle, snuffle," went Lucas.
"Huh, huh," sighed Willow.

Then while the dreamers lay sleeping, softly,
silently, came the . . .

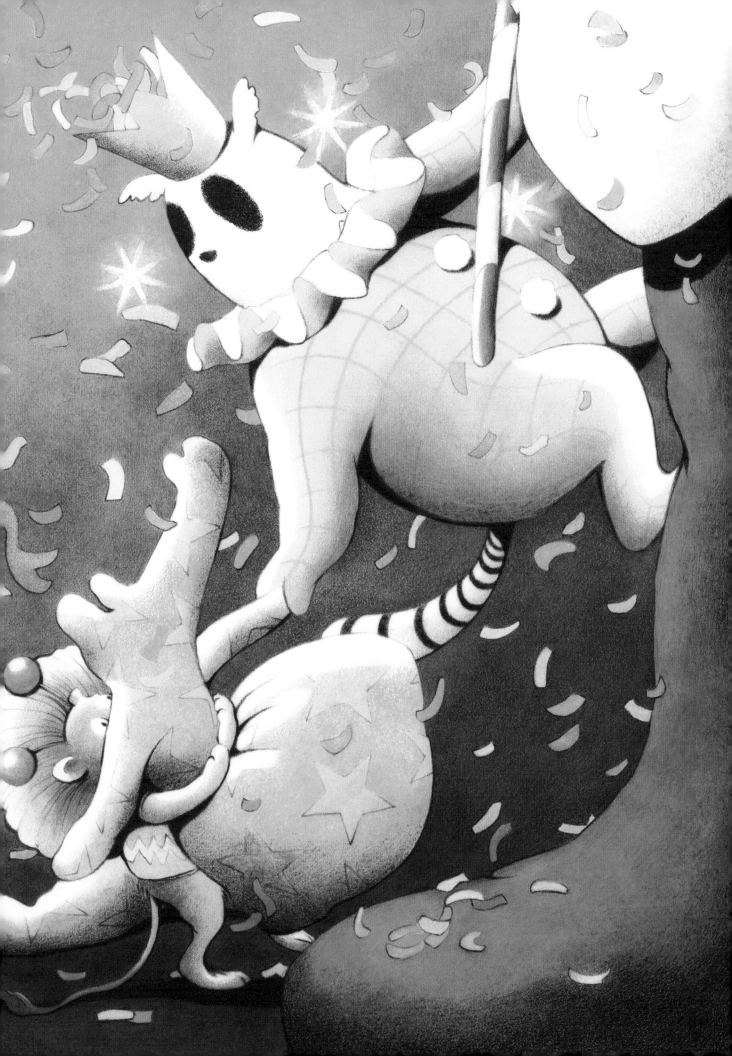

And, in a blink, on that cold winter morning, Lucas and Willow woke up and sprang to the end of their beds.

YES! It was really, really . . .

CHRISTMAS!

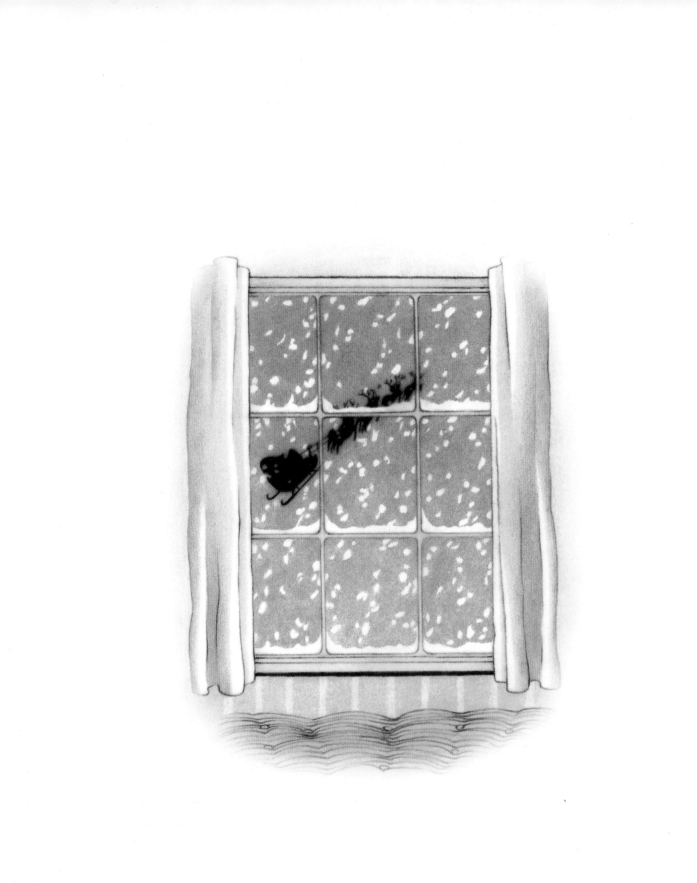